AT THE HOTEL LARRY

Daniel Pinkwater

Illustrated by
Jill Pinkwater

MARSHALL CAVENDISH
New York • London • Singapore

2006

W9-CBS-190

McCORMICKS CREEK ELEMENTARY

LARRY

is a polar bear. Once, in Bayonne, New
Jersey, he saved my father's life. My father
was grateful. He told Larry he would give
him anything he wanted as a reward.
Larry said that he wanted to live in a hotel
with a swimming pool. So my father
bought an old hotel with a pool. He named
it the Hotel Larry. That is why we live in
a hotel instead of a house or an apartment
like most people.

The pool is in a big room in the basement of the Hotel Larry. My father keeps the water very cold. Larry likes that. There is a sign outside the door to the swimming pool room:

NOTICE TO ALL GUESTS:
MAKE SURE THE
BEAR LIKES YOU
BEFORE USING
THE POOL.

My mother works in the hotel. She stands behind the front
desk. Guests ask her, "How can we tell if the bear likes us?"
My mother says, "Oh, the bear likes almost everybody."
Very few guests use the pool.

I use the pool. I swim with Larry every day. Larry is my friend. I am used to the cold water.

I am a good swimmer. I can do fifty laps. Larry taught me. Larry can do one thousand laps. Sometimes, Larry lets me ride on his back or his stomach. And we have a big ball we toss back and forth.

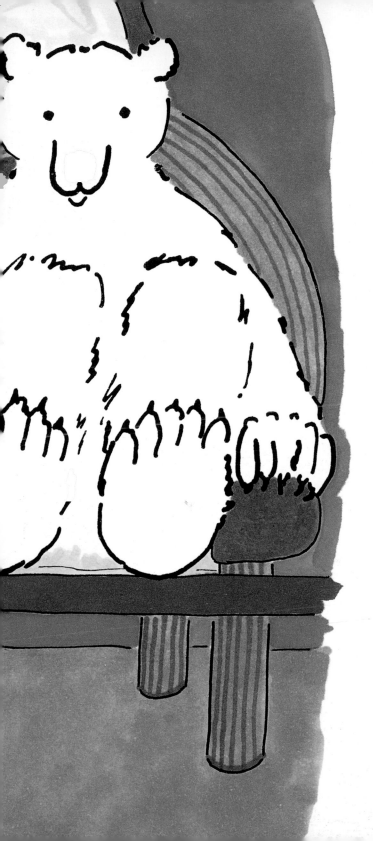

Once I asked Larry if it was true that polar bears sometimes eat people.

Larry said, "I am ashamed to say that it is true. But I am sure any bear who has eaten a person had a very good reason. I myself have never done such a thing, of course."

"Of course," I said.

Larry likes it when I take him out for blueberry pancakes. He has promised my father that he will not leave the hotel unless I go with him. We go to the Pancake Palace.

I found a very large coat for Larry. I also found him a hat and sunglasses. This is what he wears when we go out. I don't do anything about Larry's feet. People think he is just a big fat man with whiskers, wearing a pair of those slippers that look like fuzzy bear paws.

If anyone were to ask I would say that Larry is my uncle from Milwaukee.

One time, when we were at the Pancake Palace, eating our blueberry pancakes, we decided to go to the zoo. It was not far. We could walk there.

Larry liked the zoo. "Why have we never come here before?" he asked.

Larry liked the monkeys. He thought they were funny. He also liked the zebras and the African lions.

"Are these animals good to eat?" he asked.

"No," I said. "It is against the law to eat a lion."

Then we saw the polar bears. "Well I will
be a cross-eyed penguin with a bent beak!"
Larry said. "Do you know who that is
in the pool?"

"No. Who?" I asked.

"That is my brother Roy!" Larry said. "Hey,
Roy! You old blubber-head! Look who's here!"

Larry said to me, "Hold my coat and hat. I am going
to jump in the pool and talk to Roy."

"Larry, they are wild polar bears," I said.

"I am a wild polar bear myself," Larry said. "There is no
other kind."

Larry jumped into the polar bear pool.

"What if someone notices there are four polar bears instead of the usual three?" I called to him.

"Hey, look! It's Roy! Wave to Roy!" Larry said.

I waved to Roy. Roy waved back.

People walked up to the polar bear pool. "Oh, look! Look at the polar bears!" they said. "Take a picture."

Larry and his brother, Roy, and the two other polar bears faced the people and smiled big smiles.

The people took their pictures, looked at the bears for a while, and walked away. Nobody seemed to notice that there were four bears instead of the usual three.

Finally, Larry climbed out of the pool, up the steep side of the polar bear area, and over the fence.

"That was fun," he said. "I never thought I'd meet my brother here."

"You got out without any trouble," I said. "Why can't the other bears do that?"

"They can," he said. "They are coming to supper at the Hotel Larry."

"We have to ask my mother and father," I said.

"And we have to find three big coats, and hats," Larry said.

My mother and father said it would be fine for Larry's brother, Roy, and their polar bear friends to have supper at the Hotel Larry. My mother asked Larry what the polar bears would like to eat.

"Codfish cakes," Larry said. "And blueberries."

"Will they want to swim?" my father asked.

"I am sure they will want to swim," Larry said.

"I will put ice in the pool," my father said.

That night, Larry and I went to the zoo. We waited by the gate. We had three very big coats, three hats, and three pairs of sunglasses, even though it was night.

The bears arrived at the gate. They were with a zookeeper. The zookeeper unlocked the gate. "Please sign this," the zookeeper said. He handed me a piece of paper:

> Received: three (3) polar bears, Roy, Bear Number One, and Bear Number Three. To be returned to the zoo in good condition.
>
> sign here_____

I signed my name.

The bears put on the coats and hats and sunglasses. We began walking to the Hotel Larry.

On the way, we passed a policeman. "They are my four uncles from Milwaukee," I said.

At the Hotel Larry the bears had a good time. They put blueberries on their codfish cakes. Larry and Roy told stories of the time they were cubs. Bear Number One and Bear Number Three told stories about life in the zoo.

None of the bears had ever eaten a person.

After supper we waited a half-hour. Bear Number One and
Bear Number Three and my father smoked cigars. Larry and
Roy helped me clear the table. My mother played songs on
the piano.

Then we all went for a swim.

To each other,
D. P. and J. P.

Text copyright © 1997 by Daniel Pinkwater
Illustrations copyright © 1997 by Jill Pinkwater
All rights reserved.
Marshall Cavendish, 99 White Plains Road, Tarrytown, NY 10591
www.marshallcavendish.com
The text of this book is set in 16 point Esprit Book.
The illustrations are rendered in pen and ink and colored markers.
Printed in Hong Kong
First Marshall Cavendish paperback edition, 2004
1 3 5 6 4 2

Library of Congress Cataloging-in-Publication Data Pinkwater, Daniel Manus.
At the Hotel Larry / Daniel Pinkwater; illustrated by Jill Pinkwater p. cm. Summary: A young
girl and Larry, the polar bear who lives in her father's hotel, enjoy each other's company and, on an
outing to the zoo, they discover Larry's brother Roy. ISBN 0-7614-5178-1
[1. Polar bear—Fiction. 2. Bears—Fiction. 3. Humorous stories.] I. Pinkwater, Jill, ill. II. Title.
PZ7.P6335Arp   1998   [E]—dc20   96–41671   CIP   AC